Bedtime Wishes
睡前願望

Jonathan Augustine　著

Machi Takagi　繪

三民書局

國家圖書館出版品預行編目資料

Bedtime Wishes:睡前願望 / Jonathan Augustine著;
Machi Takagi繪;本局編輯部譯.－－初版一刷.－
－臺北市：三民，2005
面；　公分.－－(愛閱雙語叢書.世界故事集系
列)
中英對照
ISBN 957-14-4233-X　（平裝）

1.英國語言－讀本

805.18　　　　　　　　　　　94001423

網路書店位址　http://www.sanmin.com.tw

© **Bedtime Wishes**
　　——睡前願望

著作人　　Jonathan Augustine
繪　者　　Machi Takagi
譯　者　　本局編輯部
發行人　　劉振強
著作財
產權人　　三民書局股份有限公司
　　　　　臺北市復興北路386號
發行所　　三民書局股份有限公司
　　　　　地址／臺北市復興北路386號
　　　　　電話／(02)25006600
　　　　　郵撥／0009998-5
印刷所　　三民書局股份有限公司
門市部　　復北店／臺北市復興北路386號
　　　　　重南店／臺北市重慶南路一段61號
初版一刷　2005年2月
編　號　　S 805170
定　價　　新臺幣貳佰參拾元整
行政院新聞局登記證局版臺業字第○二○○號

有著作權·不准侵害

ISBN　957-14-4233-X　（平裝）

TO OUR BELOVED DAUGHTERS
MAYU AND YUMI

David lay grumbling in bed—it just wasn't fair!

His older brother Matt wouldn't let him use his dartboard. His mother griped that he'd made holes in the wall. Later at dinner his father had scolded him for blowing bubbles in his milk.

All alone in his room now, he looked at the painted stars and moon that glowed down on him from the ceiling and made a wish that the world would leave him alone.

Next morning the sunshine smiled brightly into his room as David awoke from a comfortable dream. He rubbed his sleepy eyes and was surprised to see it was already nine.

"What's wrong with the alarm clock?" he roared.

But when he climbed to the upper bunk, instead of finding his brother smothered in untidy covers, he found only George the stuffed lion, sound asleep.

"Mommm!" he shook the house with his voice. "Is today a holiday?"

In his outgrown pajamas David rushed through the rooms but found them all empty. Then he dashed outside and down the block that was usually full of joggers and cars by this time. But for some reason there was no sign of life. Even old Mrs. Baker, who always sat in her rocking chair, was not out on her porch.

"Wow, I'm really all alone!" David shouted with delight.

One shoe off and one shoe on, David raced back through the house and opened his brother's closet where the precious dartboard lay hidden under some clothes. With great satisfaction, David tossed all of his brother's darts and only made two holes in the wall.

After a morning of romping about the empty house, his stomach suddenly growled.

"No bacon and eggs for me," he said, dragging up a stool over to reach the freezer.

"Chocolate chip, mint or raspberry.... They all sound good for breakfast!" he shouted in delight. And in a large bowl he stacked five scoops of ice cream with caramel sauce, whipped cream and a cherry on top. Then he found the hidden cookie jar his mother said was only for "good boys and girls."

After such a scrumptious breakfast, David lay in his father's great big armchair watching all the cartoons he would have missed ordinarily if he were at school.

"I wonder if there's anybody downtown?" David asked himself. So he jumped on his bike to take a look. Along the way he saw vacant shops with toys and clothes on display in the windows. But wherever he looked, there was not a person in sight.

When he passed the grocery store he said, "Maybe I'll need some more food."

So he rode down the aisles on the grocery cart picking out his favorite cookies, potato chips, candy bars, and magazines. "I'll buy some apples and bananas too."

On the way home, he passed by the zoo and saw the gates open with no ticket collector in sight, so of course he went right in. Holding up his bag of mouth-watering treats, David stuck his tongue out at the hungry lion as he passed by.

LION

His favorite spot was always the monkey pit. Today, the monkeys were chasing each other, trying to capture an abandoned little red shoe. But they dropped the shoe when they saw the bananas in David's bag.

"Mom won't be happy if I give you guys the only things I bought that are good for me," David hesitated. But since the monkeys were jumping up and down, David gave in and threw the bananas into the pit.

While the monkeys were busy eating the bananas, David crossed over the wall that surrounded the monkey pit. Then he climbed to the top of the monkey mountain and played on their swings. But after a while, the bananas were gone and David grew tired of being a monkey.

On his way home, he decided to stop by the playground. But when he arrived at the park, his friends were not there playing baseball. The kids making sand castles were not there either.

When David arrived home he cried out, "Mom, Dad, I'm home!"

But there was no reply. He couldn't hear his mom humming her cheerful tune as she chopped vegetables. His dad wasn't listening to the radio either. He wished someone would reply—even his bossy brother would be okay.

Instead of fixing supper, David went straight to his room and tucked George the lion into his covers. And with a mournful look, he stared at the stars on his ceiling and whispered, "Oh, I'll promise to be good from now on, so would you please all come back? I want shouting, laughter and confusion."

But before he finished his sentence, he was sound asleep.

At seven in the morning, David jumped out of bed to the ringing sound of the alarm clock. He heard his brother grumble a few sleepy words, so he raced up the ladder to the upper bunk and shouted, "Oh, it's so good to see you, scruffy head. You just won't believe what happened yesterday."

But before his brother could make sense out of David's words, David dashed out of the bedroom.

David's mother and father were setting the table when he entered the kitchen.

"You got up by yourself," his mother greeted him with a smile.

"Mom, Dad, I'm so glad you're back. Don't ever leave me again, okay?"

"Don't be silly, we've never left you, even for a day," exclaimed his father in astonishment.

David looked confused for a second. But he forgot about everything when he saw what was for breakfast.

"Bacon and eggs. Mmmm!" he shouted with delight.

難字註解

p.2
dartboard [ˈdɑrtˌbɔrd] n. 飛鏢的鏢靶
gripe [graɪp] v. 抱怨，發牢騷

p.4
bunk [bʌŋk] n.（雙層床的）床鋪
smother [ˈsmʌðɚ] v. 用…覆蓋

p.8
satisfaction [ˌsætɪsˈfækʃən] n. 滿足，滿意
toss [tɔs] v. 扔

p.10
caramel [ˈkærəml̩] n. 焦糖

p.12
scrumptious [ˈskrʌmpʃəs] adj.（食物）非常
　　　　　　　　　　　　　　　好吃的

p.14
vacant [ˈvekənt] adj.（房間、座位、房子等）
　　　　　　　　　　　　　　空的
display [dɪˈsple] v. 展示，陳列
grocery store　雜貨店

故事中譯

⭐ *p.2* ⭐

大衛躺在床上抱怨：「這真是不公平！」

哥哥麥特不肯借他飛鏢靶；媽媽因為大衛在牆上弄了些洞而唸他；然後晚餐時，爸爸也因為他在牛奶裡吹泡泡而罵他。

現在，大衛單獨在房間裡，看著畫在天花板上、對著他發亮的星星和月亮，許下了一個願望──希望全世界只剩下他一個人。

⭐ *p.4* ⭐

第二天早上，當大衛從一個舒服的好夢中醒來時，燦爛的陽光已經照亮了他的房間。大衛揉揉惺忪的睡眼，驚訝的發現竟然已經九點了！

他大吼：「鬧鐘怎麼沒響啊？」

可是當他爬到床的上鋪時，卻沒看到哥哥裹在亂七八糟的棉被裡，只發現看來睡得很甜的填充玩具獅子，喬治。

大衛以足以震動整間屋子的聲音大喊：「媽！今天放假嗎？」

⭐ *p.6* ⭐

大衛穿著有點太小的睡衣匆匆跑過每個房間，卻發現屋內空無一人！於是他再衝出家門，卻看到平常的這個時候，應該已經充滿慢跑的人和車輛的街道，不知什麼緣故，現在竟然也連一個人影都沒有！就連總是在自己家門廊坐著搖椅的貝克老太太，也不見蹤影了。

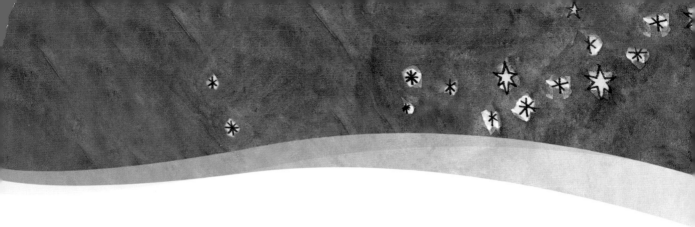

☆ *p.8* ☆

　　腳上只剩一隻鞋的大衛衝回家裡，打開哥哥的衣櫥，翻出藏在衣服堆下的寶貝飛鏢靶。然後，大衛把哥哥的飛鏢通通射到靶上過足了癮，而且只在牆上弄出了兩個洞喔！

☆ *p.10* ☆

　　在空盪盪的家裡蹦蹦跳跳的玩了整個早上後，大衛的肚子忽然咕嚕咕嚕作響。

　　大衛說：「沒人弄培根和蛋給我吃。」他拖來一張矮凳子墊腳，打開冷凍庫，開心的大叫：「有巧克力碎片、薄荷跟覆盆子口味的冰淇淋……嗯，它們都很適合當早餐！」他在一個大碗裡堆了五球冰淇淋，淋上焦糖、鮮奶油，最上面還放了顆櫻桃。接著，大衛還找到了一罐被媽媽藏起來、說只給「乖孩子」吃的餅乾。

☆ *p.12* ☆

　　吃完這頓超好吃的早餐後，大衛躺在爸爸大大的扶手椅上，看了所有平常上學時錯過的卡通。

☆ *p.14* ☆

　　大衛自言自語：「不知道市中心有沒有人？」於是他跳上腳踏車，決定去瞧瞧。一路上，大衛看到許多空的商店，櫥窗裡展示著玩具和衣服。可是無論他往哪裡看，就是看不到半個人影。

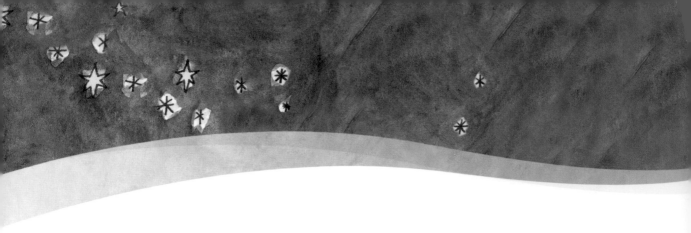

經過雜貨店時，大衛說：「我可能會需要多一點食物。」

於是大衛推著購物車穿梭在走道間，挑選他最愛的餅乾、洋芋片、糖果棒，還有幾本雜誌。他想：「再買些蘋果和香蕉好了。」

⭐ *p.16* ⭐

回家途中，大衛經過動物園時，看到大門開著，又不見收票員的蹤影，所以，他當然就大搖大擺的進去逛逛囉！大衛手上拿著他那袋令人口水直流的美食，在經過獅籠的時候，還對著饑餓的獅子吐舌頭呢！

⭐ *p.18* ⭐

大衛一向最喜歡猿猴區了。今天，猴子們互相追來追去的，在搶一隻被丟棄的小紅鞋。可是當他們一看到大衛袋子裡的香蕉，就把小紅鞋丟到一邊去了。

大衛猶豫著：「如果我把今天買的東西裡唯一對我有益的給你們，媽媽會不高興的。」不過看到猴子們跳上跳下的，最後大衛還是投降了，把香蕉丟給了猴子們。

⭐ *p.20* ⭐

正當猴子們忙著吃香蕉時，大衛攀過了猿猴區的圍牆，爬到猴山頂端，玩起了牠們的鞦韆。然而過了一會兒，香蕉被吃完了，而大衛也對當猴子感到厭煩了。

⭐ *p.26* ⭐

　　大衛沒有準備晚餐，反而直接走進他的房間，蓋上棉被，並把獅子喬治緊緊抱在懷裡。他悶悶不樂的盯著天花板上的星星看，低聲說：「喔，我保證從現在起都會乖乖的，請你們都回來好嗎？我好想念那些叫聲、笑聲，還有混亂和騷動……」不過話還沒說完，大衛就睡著了。

⭐ *p.28* ⭐

　　早上七點時，大衛一聽到鬧鐘響起就跳下床。聽到哥哥嘀咕了幾句夢話，大衛很快的爬上梯子，對著睡在上鋪的哥哥喊：「喔，看到你真好，邋遢鬼！你一定不會相信昨天發生了什麼事！」

　　在哥哥聽懂他的話前，大衛就已經衝出房間了。

⭐ *p.30* ⭐

　　大衛進到廚房時，媽媽和爸爸正在佈置餐桌準備早餐。

　　媽媽對著大衛微笑：「你自己起床了呢！」

　　「爸、媽，看到你們回來真好。以後不要再離開我了，好嗎？」

　　爸爸驚愕的叫著：「別傻了，我們從來沒離開過你，就連一天也沒有啊！」

　　大衛困惑的表情只持續了一秒鐘。當他看到早餐的菜色時，馬上就忘光了所有疑問。

　　他大聲歡呼：「喔耶！是培根蛋耶！」

Exercise

Look at the pictures and write the missing words. They all come from the story.

1. We usually go to the  once a week for our daily

   necessities. _____

2. Dad climbed up the to change the light bulb.

   _____

3. The in the park is popular with families with young

   children. _____

4. Last night I accidentally fell to the ground from the upper

    and twisted my ankle. _____

5. A  is a long, narrow, sweet food, usually covered in

   chocolate. _____

38

Understanding the Story

Choose the correct words to complete the sentences. Tick (✓) A, B, C, or D.

1. David made a wish that
- ☐ A. his brother would give him the dartboard.
- ☐ B. the world would leave him alone.
- ☐ C. he could have ice cream for breakfast.
- ☐ D. he could blow bubbles in his milk.

2. When David woke up the next morning, he found that
- ☐ A. he was late for school.
- ☐ B. the breakfast was ready for him.
- ☐ C. the house was full of people.
- ☐ D. all his families were gone.

3. David spent the day alone; he
- ☐ A. shopped at the grocery store and went to the zoo.
- ☐ B. slept all day long.
- ☐ C. had his hair cut and bought some new clothes.
- ☐ D. was too sad to do anything.

4. After spending the day all alone, David felt
- ☐ A. happy.
- ☐ B. angry.
- ☐ C. embarrassed.
- ☐ D. lonely.

5. In the end,

☐A. David could not find his family.

☐B. David was disappointed to find that his breakfast were bacon and eggs.

☐C. David's families all came back and David felt very happy.

☐D. David was unhappy to see his brother.

 Questions for You!

1. Have you ever wished that people of the world, including your families, would disappear? Why?

2. What would you do first if people of the world, including your families, disappeared?

3. What would you do if you didn't get along well with your families just as David did in the story?

 Answers

作者／繪者簡介

　　Machi Takagi and Jonathan Augustine have traveled throughout the world as husband and wife. They devote much of their time toward artistically expressing their fascination with cultural diversity. Machi Takagi is a painter of *nihonga* (traditional Japanese painting) and Jonathan Augustine is a professor of international communication at the Kyoto Institute of Technology in Japan.

　　作者Jonathan Augustine博士與繪者Machi Takagi女士夫婦的足跡遍佈世界各地。他們為文化的多樣性深深著迷，並藉著藝術形式記錄對各種文化的感情。 Machi Takagi女士為 「傳統日本畫」(nihonga)畫家，而Jonathan Augustine博士現為日本京都工藝纖維大學國際傳播教授。

愛閱雙語叢書

黛安的日記
Diane's Diary

Ronald Brown　著

呂亨英　　　　譯

劉俊男　莊孝先　繪

中英雙語，附CD

想知道台灣女孩在美國生活，
會發生什麼事嗎？
看黛安的日記就知道了！

不得了了！在台灣土生土長的黛安，居然因為爸爸工作的關係，要跟全家人一起移民美國！日記就從放暑假的第一天開始，紀錄黛安一家人在美國生活、黛安參加夏令營等趣事。看黛安如何用輕鬆活潑的口吻，跟讀者分享她的新生活。

愛閱雙語叢書

給愛兒的二十封信
Letters to My Son

簡　宛 著

簡宛・石廷・Dr. Jane Vella 譯

杜曉西 繪

中英雙語，附CD

本書集結二十封作者給兒子的家書，作者以風趣流暢的筆觸，取代傳統說教方式，字裡行間盡是母親對兒子的關愛之情及殷殷期盼。這本溫馨且充滿母愛的中英對照書信集，為成千上萬的父母與青少年提供了最佳的溝通管道，也是最好的「悅讀」及學習英文的方式。

二十篇母子間的心靈對談
二十封溫馨感人的書信